Kate McKinnon

PUFFIN

BEFORE YO

Before You Grow Up is
original poems for younge
who can still share and enjoy the fun and fantasies of
childhood. There are short, snappy nonsense rhymes,
narrative verse in the tradition of Hilaire Belloc and a
wise look at life as children see it. Fresh, accessible
language and rhythms make this an ideal book for
reading aloud to young children and for children to
learn to read for themselves. Finola Akister success-
fully combines the world of the exotic with that of the
everyday, for in this book it's not that surprising for
elephants to turn up for tea (even if they are uninvited)
or for you to meet a tiger walking down the street. Cer-
tainly you have to prepare for the most unexpected
things to happen!

Before You Grow Up is Finola Akister's first book
of poetry for children and, in fact, her first book to
be published. The poems were originally written to
entertain her two grandsons. Finola Akister lives in
Buckinghamshire. Colin West is well known as a writer
and collector of nonsense and verse as well as a popular
comic illustrator.

Before you grow up

Poems by Finola Akister

Illustrated by Colin West

PUFFIN BOOKS

PUFFIN BOOKS

Published by the Penguin Group
27 Wrights Lane, London W8 5TZ, England
Viking Penguin Inc., 40 West 23rd Street, New York, New York 10010, USA
Penguin Books Australia Ltd, Ringwood, Victoria, Australia
Penguin Books Canada Ltd, 2801 John Street, Markham, Ontario, Canada L3R 1B4
Penguin Books (NZ) Ltd, 182–190 Wairau Road, Auckland 10, New Zealand

Penguin Books Ltd, Registered Offices: Harmondsworth, Middlesex, England

First published by Viking Kestrel 1987
Published in Puffin Books 1989
1 3 5 7 9 10 8 6 4 2

Printed and bound in Great Britain by
Cox & Wyman Ltd, Reading
Filmset in Century Schoolbook

A butterfly just fluttered by
And settled on a rose.
Where it came from I don't know,
I cannot say where it will go,
For suddenly it flew away.
But still, I'm glad it came today.

Always it amazes me
How slippery the soap can be.
I pick it up and start to rub,
When WHOOSH – it jumps into the tub.
I search and search and search around:
That bar of soap just can't be found.
Instead of lying in the dish,
It's swimming round, just like a fish.
I cannot catch it – golly gosh,
I think I'll go without a wash.

It was early in the morning,
Just as the day was dawning,
That Fido packed his bone and ran away.
But, realizing what he'd done,
He thought it wasn't much like fun,
So he turned about and hurried home next day.

Cats like milk.

Mice like cheese.

Little dogs like sausagees.

Crabs always walk sideways, and so
Spare a thought for this unhappy plight.
If a left-handed crab always walked to the left,
And his true love was geared to the right,

They would pass by like ships in the night.
Just a wave as they hove into view,
Destined never to walk side by side, or to talk
Claw in claw, like the other crabs do.

The solution is not hard to find,
And matters could be so much worse –
There's the chance they could meet on the
  strand or the street.
If one of them walked in reverse.

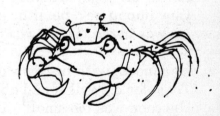

Zanzibar was a very large lion,
With a beautiful lion-like mane.
He looked very fierce, ferocious and wild,
Though, in fact, he was terribly tame.

His grandad was born in the jungle,
Where the weather was sultry and hot.
But Zanzibar knew, as he gazed round the zoo,
That, in England, the weather was not.

He thought, with his lion-like thinking,
As he lazily gazed round the zoo,
How happy he'd be, if he only were free.
He was bored. There was nothing to do.

He longed, with his lion-like longing,
To go for a stroll round about.
His cage was too small – there was no room at
  all –
But his keeper would not let him out.

Zanzibar scowled at the keeper,
In his lion-like sort of way.
Should I eat him? he thought. But he'd have to
 be caught.
And the keeper kept out of his way.

So Zanzibar lay there and brooded,
Till one day – it was just getting dark –
They hustled him into a lorry
And drove him away to a park.

Now Zanzibar gazes about him.
He is pleased with this lovely new place.
He lies on the grass with a lion-type lass
And a smile on his lion-like face.

There is one thing I cannot do
Because, you see, I'm only two.
No matter how I try and try,
It nearly always makes me cry.
I don't know when it all began,
Or why some very clever man
Thought that buttons could be fun –
I simply can't get mine undone.
My mother comes and helps me out,
But, really, what's it all about?
Although I try, it's all in vain.
I just can't do them up again.

He was small and white,
With eyes so bright,
But he wandered away from the house.
He was small and sweet,
So if you should meet,
Please bring me back my mouse.

I'll polish up the teapot, thought Sarah Jane
one night.
Mummy will be so surprised to see it shining
bright.
She found the cloth for polishing, and then, with
might and main,
She rubbed it once, and just for luck she rubbed
it once again.

Sarah Jane was worried that she hadn't done it
right,
For as she rubbed, with might and main, there
came a blinding light.
And standing there before her was a giant, ten
feet tall.
He was smiling down upon her, which made her
feel so small.

His mighty arms were folded on his very mighty
  chest.
He wore a turban on his head and jewels on his
  vest.
His shoes were just like gravy boats, and
  everybody knows

That shoes like that are always made with
funny curled-up toes.

Sarah Jane was speechless, so great was her
surprise.
She gazed upon the giant – she could not believe
her eyes.
His arms unfolded slowly, then he waved one
mighty hand:
'I am the Teapot Genie, and I wait for your
command.'

Sarah Jane had heard about the Genie of the
Ring.
She had heard about the Genie of the Lamp and
everything.
But she had never thought that teapots had a
genie too –
She'd heard of 'instant', 'quick' and 'fine' but not
of 'genie' brew.

'Please, could I have a teddy bear?' asked little
  Sarah J.
At once, with just a puff of smoke, the Genie
  went away.
Sarah Jane woke up and found that she was still
  in bed.
It must have been a dream – but what was this
  beside her head?

It was a lovely teddy bear and just exactly
  right.
She wondered where it came from 'cause it
  wasn't there last night.
It's very, very strange, and Sarah Jane cannot
  explain.
She isn't even sure herself from where her teddy
  came.

It came down from the ceiling
On a silken, single thread.
I screamed out loud
Because I don't
Like spiders in my bed.

Lots of spots

Are polka dots.

An elephant, they said, had come to see me in
the morning.
I thought it very odd that this should be.
I was surprised – no, even more, I was certain, I
was *sure*
That I didn't know an elephant, so how could
one know me?

I didn't like to tell them that I didn't know an
elephant,
So I pretended that it wasn't strange to me,
And I made it very plain that, should he ever
call again,
I'd be obliged if they would ask him in for tea.

It's very odd, they said, that I was friendly with
an elephant.
It might seem odd to them, but not to me.
They hinted I was lying and remarked, 'Perhaps
a lion
Or a hippopotamus might come along and want
some tea.'

'I am not,' I said, 'acquainted with a single
  hippopotamus,
And a lion is an animal with whom I disagree.
The monkeys that I knew are really very, very
  few,
But an elephant is different and should be asked
  to tea.'

Still I couldn't make them see that elephants
  were different.
Perhaps it's just as well, you will agree,
For I really do not know a single elephant,
  and so
They will never be obliged to ask my elephant
  to tea.

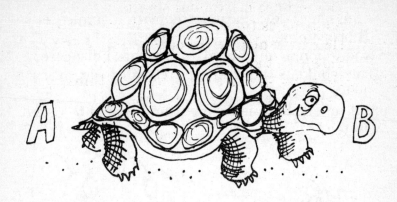

The tortoise moves, but slowly,
As he goes from A to B.
He takes his time along the way,
But what he thinks, I cannot say
Because (it's very sad to tell)
He never comes out of his shell.

He never rushes, I am told,
Or runs on recklessly.
What his pace is I don't know,
But I am certain it is slow.
Why he lingers I can't say —
It must be 'cause he's made that way.

The tortoise moves, but slowly.
It is obvious that he
Has got a heavy load to bear.
He takes it with him everywhere.
The house he carries on his back
Must be a heavy handicap.

The tortoise moves, but slowly,
As he plods from A to B.
He crawls along from day to day,
Slowly but surely on his way.
He stops – I don't know what he thinks.
Perhaps he's having forty winks.

Yes, the tortoise moves so slowly:
He seems to lack the pace.
I asked him, was he good or bad,
Was he happy, was he sad?
He said he didn't want to tell,
And disappeared inside his shell.

The tortoise does not move at all
From A or B or C.
It's winter, and the snow came down.
He didn't laugh or smile or frown
But, slow and steady, he did creep
Into his shell, and fell asleep.

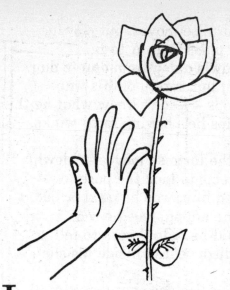

I saw a lovely rose one day,
As I was passing on my way,
But when I tried to pick it, oh,
It pricked my little finger so.
I will not pick a rose again.
Instead I'll make a daisy chain.

My bedroom gets into a mess.
I tidy up and then
The next day it is just as bad,
So I tidy up again.

If I could choose
What I would be,
I'd like to be a bumble bee.
I'd bumble in and out of flowers,
But only during sunny hours,
For if it rained hard, you can bet
I'd bumble off and not get wet.

When I was just a foal,
My mother said to me,
'Always do as you are told,
And never disagree.'
I'd like to do just as she said –
There isn't any doubt –
But whenever I open my mouth to say, 'Yes,'
It's always a 'Neigh' that comes out.

Neigh!

If, walking down a busy street,
It happens that you chance to meet
A tiger,
You must be discreet.
But
If it is a pussy cat,
By all means stop and have a chat.

30

A camel can race through the desert
Because everyone knows
He doesn't get hot,
Or bothered a lot,
By sand between his toes.

You have heard of the ugly duckling
Who turned into a beautiful swan.
But have you heard
Of the ugly swan
Who had rotten luck
And didn't turn into
A beautiful duck?

They look like little baskets,
Hanging up there in the tree.
I know that they are birds' nests,
But I think you will agree
That if their owners spent more time
And built a little roof,
Nests really would be warmer
And much more weather-proof.

The mule is a beast of burden.
He is strong, but he's obstinate too.
If he's bearing a grudge,
And unwilling to budge,
There is nothing at all you can do.

Just when I thought I had made it,
And it really was looking so grand,
I picked up my model kit aeroplane –
Then it all fell apart in my hand.

I wash my face – that's easy –
Though sometimes I have fears:
Mum says she could grow potatoes
In the space behind my ears.

I've thought and thought about it,.
And it might be just as well,
If I took some care, while the soap is there,
To wash that space as well.

When we go on a trip to the seaside,
My mum and dad take my hand.
Because it's in reach, we go down to the beach
And make castles with buckets of sand.

Mum takes a case to this heavenly place.
It is packed tight with goodies to eat.
Dad digs a hole, with the zest of a mole,
Then the tide comes and tickles my feet.

But when we get home to the garden,
Dad's fervour for digging is slack.
He puts down the spade, goes and sits in the
   shade
And explains that he's got a bad back.

The tide comes in
Upon the shore.
It turns about.
The tide goes out.

I have a lovely car, you know.
I get in it and go, go, go.
Near and far, up and down,
I travel all around the town.
I toot my horn (it's only fair
To let the people know I'm there).
Even on hills I do not shirk,
Though pedalling up hills is hard work.

I try not to paddle in puddles,
And I try to eat cabbage as well.
I try to be good 'cause I know that I should,
So why I am bad I can't tell.

It's just that a puddle is tempting,
And cabbage, I think, is a mess.
I'll have to start walking round puddles
And swallow the cabbage, I guess.

They tell me an elephant never forgets,
And, of course, what they say may be so.
That's all very well, but how can they tell?
I mean, how can they possibly know?

The extraordinary thing about daisies –
I must make this abundantly plain –
Is they're mowed with the lawn
(You can't see one at all),
But the next day they're all back again.

The barn owl looked out through his spectacled
  eyes,
And he gazed at the farmyard below.
The sun was beginning to rise in the east,
And the cock was beginning to crow.
It is time, thought the owl, I was going to sleep.
He was old, he was wise and he knew
That for him it was right. He'd been up half the
  night
Serenading that girl owl with two things in
  sight,
Namely, to-whit and to-woo.

Dog was a stray with nowhere to stay.
He just wandered about in the street.
He spent every day in the usual way,
Just looking for something to eat.

He wasn't to blame 'cause he hadn't a name,
Though he desperately wished that he had.
He never had known a name of his own.
He was lonely and hungry and sad.

One day, without warning, at ten in the
  morning,
He walked up to a cottage and found
Something really appalling – a lady had fallen
And lay in a heap on the ground.

The lady was old and she seemed very cold.
Dog had to get help, that was plain.
Without waiting to stop, he ran to the shop
And barked loudly, again and again.

'It's that black-and-white stray. I will chase him
   away,'
Said a tall man who looked very grand.
But a woman said, 'Stay, he is trying to say
Something we don't understand.'

'I think that I know,' said the man. 'Let us go.'
Then they followed Dog out of the door.
The old lady they found. She was still on the
  ground –
She was lying there, just as before.

There was a bump on her head, so they put her
  to bed,
And soon she recovered and cried,
'How lucky am I that you chanced to pass by.
But for you I would surely have died.'

'It was not just by chance,' said the man, with a
  glance
At the lady who lay in the bed.

' 'Twas the stray dog that cried, brought us here
  to your side,
So you really should thank him instead.'

Then the old lady knew what she wanted to do,
And she smiled. It was lovely to see.
'If the dog is a stray, don't send him away.
Bring him in. He shall live here with me.'

Dog has got his desire as he lies by the fire,
For the days of his hardship are past.
He is pleased to claim that he now has a name:
It is Ben, and he's happy at last.

Humpty Dumpty sat on a wall.
He fell, so now I can see
Why all the king's horses
And all the king's men
Had scrambled egg for tea.

Jack and Jill walked up the hill,
Then they had to stop.
There was nowhere else for them to go —
They had reached the very top.

They take me here,
They take me there,
They take me almost everywhere.
But wherever they take me,
Wherever I roam,
I'm just a homing pigeon,
So I am going home.

If you should see a little dog
(He's sort of black, but here and there,
Just mixed amongst the black,
You'll find odd spots of brownish hair),

Perhaps he isn't really lost.
He just strayed off the other day.
I'm certain that he would come home
If only he could find his way.

I do not wish to be a fish.
I might end up upon a dish.
But, worse than that, if I should linger,
I might become a fried fish finger.

The good things are bad,
If you see what I mean,
Like chocolates and toffees
And cakes full of cream.
They are bad for your teeth,
And they make you grow fat,
Then they spoil your complexion.
Just think about that.

The Vikings sailed across the sea.
Each man pulled upon his oar.
Without a doubt they were all tired out
When they reached the foreign shore.

After a rest they fought with zest.
They won but, alas and alack,
They had to stay — there was no other way.
They were all too tired to row back.

They said that there were fairies at the bottom
  of the garden,
And I thought I'd go along so I could see
Just what a fairy looked like, 'cause I'd never
  come across one,
And I really longed to see just how a fairy ought
  to be.

Though I didn't see a fairy at the bottom of the
  garden
(So what a fairy looks like I really cannot say),
I think perhaps they do live at the bottom of the
  garden
But now, because it's summer, they've gone off
  on holiday.

I'm looking out the window.
I'm feeling kind of blue.
I've played at trains and lots of games,
Now I don't know what to do.
The cat's gone out. Without a doubt,
She's catching mice again.
The puppy dog has gone to sleep.
I wish it would not rain.

I've read the jolly comic book
I got from Auntie Kit.
I've tried to do the jigsaw,
But the pieces will not fit.
I've been and asked my mother
If she'd like to come and play,
But she says she's much too busy.
And the rain won't go away.

I've chatted to the goldfish,
But it doesn't make a sound.
It really doesn't do a thing
Except swim round and round.
Oh, how I wish that somebody
Would come along and play,
And how I want the sun to shine
And chase the rain away.

When it was my birthday,
Daddy asked what I would choose
For a special birthday present,
So I answered, 'Dancing shoes.'

We went to town to buy some,
But they cost an awful lot.
'Have you any cheaper?' Daddy asked,
But that was all they'd got.

So Daddy had to pay the price,
Though he made an awful fuss.
'I'm glad you're a little girl,' he said,
'And not an octopus.'

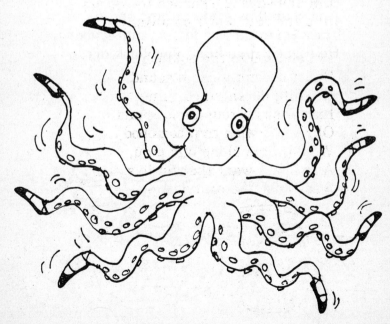

An eagle flew out of his eyrie,
And soared over mountains and plain,
Then when he was feeling quite weary,
He turned round and flew back again.

My roller skates won't ever do
The simple things I want them to.
I put them on and try my best,
But one goes East and the other goes West.

I often fall upon the floor,
Then, full of pluck, I try once more.
But my roller skates think they know best:
One still goes East and the other goes West.

Should you wish to see a crocodile,
You'll find one swiming in the Nile.
But think before you seek one out –
Their manners leave much room for doubt.
They're slinky creatures, full of guile,
And have a most preposterous smile.
I've heard it said, and think it's true,
There are some dreadful things they do.
They care not what or who you are
And are not too particular
About the menu for their tea –
They eat up anything they see.

So if, by chance, it happens you
Are wondering what is best to do,
Don't paddle near this carnivore
But safely stay upon the shore.
Throw him a bun or two and say,
'Good morning, how are you today?'
But take my warning. Do not forget:
Never keep one as a pet.

A mother bird sat in the nest
And said to her fledglings, 'Cheep, cheep.'
Roughly translated, her words meant this:
You must look before you leap.

Rings go round,
Squares are square,

But whirlygigs
Go everywhere.

If you stumble and tumble,

And you're not very tall,

You won't have very far to fall.

Will you give me a clue
As to what I should do
When I'm sent up to bed without tea?
Do I sit there and cry?
Or look out at the sky?
Oh why does this happen to me?
It's no good being haughty –
I really was naughty.
I should never have eaten that jam.
And I have to confess,
I made rather a mess
When I carved up the rest of the ham.
But when all's done and said
I sit here on my bed . . .
I'll be better tomorrow I vow.
But consider my plight:
I get no tea tonight,
And I'm ever so hungry right now.

If I was a cat,
I'd sit on the mat
And chat
To the mouse
Who lived in the house.
But
If I was the mouse
Who lived in the house,
I doubt if I'd feel
Like having
A chat
With the cat
Who sat on the mat.

If you should go to the Isle of Man,
And you should see a cat
Without a tail, don't be surprised,
Manx cats are made like that.

I know I have to go to bed.
I do not want to sleep,
For Santa Claus comes here tonight,
And I want to have a peep.

If I was very rich,
I'd walk into a shop.
I'd buy myself potato crisps
And then a lollipop.

I'd buy some pink ice-cream for you
And then some sweets for me.
But, alas, I am not very rich –
I've only got ten p.

Hey diddle diddle, the cat had a fiddle
And played it all day and all night.
Then, before very long, he burst into song,
Which, of course, gave the neighbours a fright.

The loud caterwauling was really appalling.
The noise rent the air like a knife.
The neighbours would hoot him. They
  threatened to shoot him.
So the cat had to run for his life.

I travel slowly, but I go
From here to there, and though I'm slow,
I always, always leave a trail.
I have to 'cause I am a snail.

I said I'd do my homework
(There was an awful lot),
But I forgot.
I said I'd write a thank-you note
For the present from Auntie Dot,
But I forgot.

I should have been quite sorry,
And I was, but not a lot,
'Cause I forgot.

Now I'm being good as gold,
So Mum won't be upset.
Tomorrow is my birthday.
I do hope she won't forget.

The camel has a funny lump,
Which everybody calls a hump.
He carries it upon his back.
It's like a sort of storage pack.
So he can live a long, long time
Without the need to stop and dine.
In deserts, if you stop to think,
There's nowhere he can get a drink,
And as the sun is very hot,
He's happy with the hump he's got.

He is just a fluffy chicken.
He is only one day old.
His beak is sort of yellow.
The rest of him is gold.
'Cheep, cheep,' is all he says.
It doesn't mean a lot.
But it's all that he can utter.
It's all the speech he's got.

He said his name was Walter.
He was a cross-bred hound.
He read the 'Welcome' on the mat,
So he wandered in to have a chat.
He told them he was just a stray,
And said that he would like to stay,
So Walter never went away.

I have ten fingers and ten toes.
It's just the right amount.
Apart from other useful things,
They help me when I count.

Is Archibald just a cat?
An ordinary tabby cat?
No! Archibald is more than that.

He has the habits, it is true,
Of doing things that most cats do,
But Archibald is something new . . .

Archibald belongs to me,
Which makes him special, don't you see?
I love him so, and he loves me.

I don't remember being one
Because I was so very young.
Then being two I don't recall

Because I was still very small.
The nicest year of all is three
'Cause now I can remember me.

I stand and stare. I can't believe
I'm seeing what I see.
A cow, dressed in a jumper,
Is walking straight at me.

Though odd, I agree, I'm beginning to see
The reason for it now.
The cow is wearing a jumper
Because she's a Jersey cow.

78

A bee, a very busy bee,
Was great on hospitality.
When she invited friends to dine
She gave them mead (a honey wine).
Her hive, it seemed, was not, alas,
Equipped throughout with British Gas.
There was no way that she could cook,
Nor did she have a cooking book.

Undaunted by this state of things,
She thought it out, then spread her wings.
She travelled far, she travelled near,
And then engaged a caterer.
It goes to show how much she cared –
She really was a bee prepared.

The moon peeped through the window.
I was lying in my bed.
It was very bright that starry night,
So I opened a book and read.